LOTTY'S LACE TABLE

By Tami Lehman-Wilzig

*"Enter in peace, O crown of her husband, Even in joyous song and good cheer,
Enter, O bride! Enter, O bride! Enter, O bride, the Sabbath Queen."*

Lecha Dodi (song traditionally sung Friday
night in the synagogue to welcome the Sabbath)

gefen KIDZ

**Illustrations and design
by Ksenia Topaz**

PJ Library
JEWISH BEDTIME STORIES and SONGS
www.pjlibrary.org

This
PJ BOOK
belongs to
PJ Library®
JEWISH BEDTIME STORIES and SONGS

To Sam
No one could ask for a more supportive spouse.
Thank you for always caring, pushing
and making sure that I stay on track.

Special thanks to my "reading critique community."
Judye Groner, wonderful editor, caring friend and a major force
in the field of Jewish children's literature.
Tova Teitlebaum, cousin, friend and insightful critic.
Jerry Geller, a talented man with an eye and ear for storytelling.
Judy and Ronnie Belzer, English teachers with a finger
on the pulse of today's young reader.

Illustrations and design: Ksenia Topaz

ISBN: 978–965–229–368–8

Edition 1 3 5 7 9 8 6 4 2

Gefen Publishing House, Ltd.
6 Hatzvi Street, Jerusalem 94386, Israel
972–2–538–0247 • orders@gefenpublishing.com

Gefen Books
11 Edison Place, Springfield, NJ 07081, USA
1–516–593–1234 • orders@gefenpublishing.com

www.gefenpublishing.com

Printed in Israel

Send for our free catalogue

My name is Nina. I'm very excited. Today is my mother's birthday and my grandma has given her a special present: Great-Great-Great-Grandma Lotty's famous lace tablecloth. It's the same lace tablecloth that Lotty made and sold to the Empress Elizabeth. Grandma just told me the story and I want to share it with you.

Lotty Gross, a young woman with fiery red hair, lived in Vienna at the beginning of the nineteenth century. Lotty was from a poor family and the middle child of nine, but she was determined to make a name for herself.

One day Lotty decided to take a walk through one of Vienna's wealthy neighborhoods. She couldn't help but notice the beautiful lace collars and trims of the ladies' dresses. Even the babies wore fancy lace bonnets tied under their chins, and lace booties over their chubby feet.

Lotty stopped a woman wearing a royal blue suit. Peeking out of the fitted jacket was a snowy white lace blouse with a high collar and long, flowing sleeves. "Pardon me, but where did you buy such a beautiful blouse?" Lotty asked. "I would like to get one for my mother."

"Can you afford such finery?" the woman answered.

Lotty hesitated.

"I didn't think so," smiled the lady. "Perhaps you'd like to meet my personal lace maker, Mrs. Muller. She is looking for an apprentice."

Lotty liked the idea. If she became a lace maker she might have a chance of a better marriage.
The next day Lotty set out for the lace maker's house.
"Do you have talent?" Mrs. Muller asked.
"Try me," Lotty insisted.
Mrs. Muller placed a piece of paper and a pencil on the table.
"Draw a design you think worthy of lace," she challenged Lotty.

Lotty drew a spider web and filled in small circles to represent the bugs trapped inside. Mrs. Muller pinned the pattern to a padded surface and attached several threads, each one leading to a bobbin.
"Braid the threads in pairs," she instructed.

Lotty went to work. Soon she had a small panel of lace.
"What would you like it to be?" asked the lace maker.
"A tablecloth fit for a queen," smiled Lotty.

Lotty learned quickly. The days flew into weeks, the weeks into months. Lotty created magnificent designs for blouses, evening dresses, and ball gowns. Mrs. Muller was very pleased and made Lotty her assistant. During her free time, Lotty continued to work on the tablecloth. It would be part of her wedding chest to be used every Friday evening to welcome the Sabbath Queen.

A year went by and Lotty met her husband Ruben. The first Friday after they were married, Lotty showed him the lace cloth. "Our house will be all the more beautiful when I place my candlesticks on this cloth and light the Sabbath candles," she beamed.

One day, Lotty noticed that Mrs. Muller looked pale.
"I'm afraid my health is failing," she admitted.
Lotty's eyes filled with tears. She had come to love Mrs. Muller and her work. Now it looked like she might lose both.
But Mrs. Muller was insistent. "I want the shop to stay open and I want you to run it. When I am no longer around, the business will be yours."

Ruben loved the idea of his wife running her own shop.
"Take your lace tablecloth and put it on the display table under the trims, pins, and accessories. It is your trademark," he said to Lotty.
"But I made it to welcome the Sabbath Queen," she protested.
"You can bring it home every Friday afternoon when you close shop," Ruben assured her.

Lotty did as he said.

Lotty began designing suits with matching hats, gloves, and parasols. Sometimes she dyed the lace soft pastel colors. Her lace wear became known throughout Vienna.

One day a new customer entered Lotty's shop accompanied by her maid. Dressed in a silver taffeta suit and matching hat, she looked very regal.
"May I help you?" Lotty asked.
"Are you the famous Lotty?" the woman inquired.
Lotty nodded.
"I would like to have a Lotty original as part of my wardrobe," she said while examining the pins and trims resting on top of the lace tablecloth.
"Let me show you my new designs," said Lotty, guiding her to the other side of the shop.
"Beautiful indeed," the woman fingered the garments. Then she made her way back to the tablecloth.
"I need time to think. I'll be back," she promised, as she left the store.

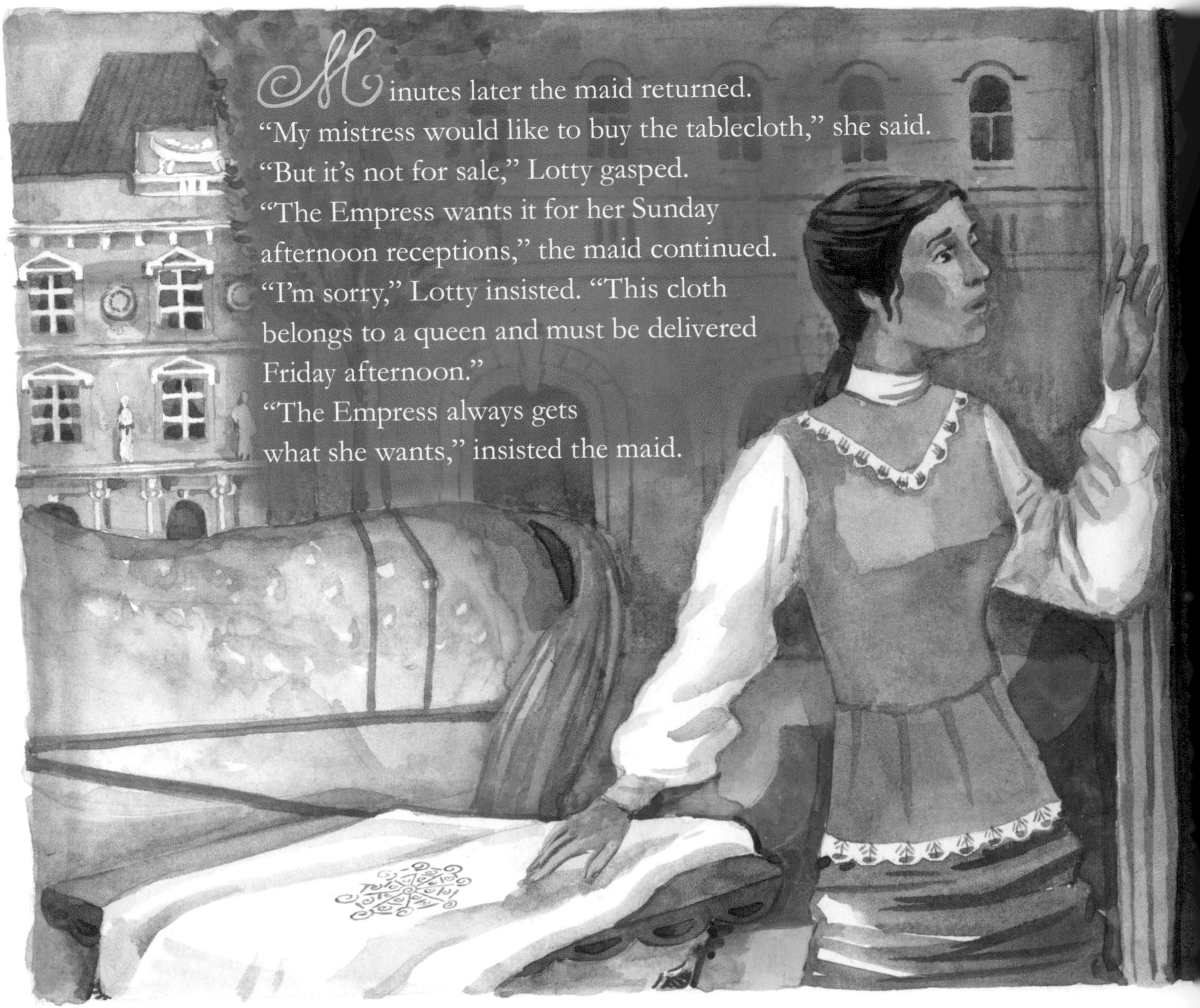

Minutes later the maid returned.
"My mistress would like to buy the tablecloth," she said.
"But it's not for sale," Lotty gasped.
"The Empress wants it for her Sunday afternoon receptions," the maid continued.
"I'm sorry," Lotty insisted. "This cloth belongs to a queen and must be delivered Friday afternoon."
"The Empress always gets what she wants," insisted the maid.

Lotty tearfully removed the tablecloth, packed it in layers of tissue paper, and brought it out to the empress's carriage.

Empress Elizabeth saw Lotty's pain. "Why is she crying over a tablecloth?" she asked as the carriage pulled away. "She said it belongs to a queen who is expecting it on Friday," answered the maid. "WHAT QUEEN!!" the empress exclaimed. "Tomorrow you must go back and find out."

Lace Shop

The next day the maid returned to Lotty's shop. She heard sobbing in the back room and the soothing voice of a man.
"Lotty, it's not the end of the world."
"I know, but I made it specially to welcome the Sabbath Queen."
Hearing this, the maid tiptoed out of the store.

"Who is the Sabbath Queen?" puzzled the empress. "Perhaps she is planning to invade the kingdom. Go again tomorrow and see what you can find out."

Once again, the maid returned to the lace shop. As she neared the store a man opened its door, hugged Lotty, then left.
"May I have a word with you?" the maid approached Ruben.
"I work for the Empress Elizabeth. She heard the lace maker talk about the Sabbath Queen and would like to invite her for tea."

Ruben laughed. "The Sabbath Queen is not a real person. The Jews refer to the Sabbath as a queen because on the Sabbath every Jewish home has a feeling of majesty."
"Why is the tablecloth so important to your wife?" asked the puzzled maid.
"Doesn't a queen deserve finery? My wife spent a year making that cloth for her wedding chest so she could use it every Friday night to welcome the Sabbath. But..." Ruben hesitated, "...she is happy to serve the empress."

That Sunday Empress Elizabeth showed off her new lace tablecloth at the palace reception. All her guests admired Lotty's beautiful handiwork. When the party was over the empress ordered her maid to carefully wrap the cloth. "Go to Lotty's shop on Friday morning. Give her the cloth. Tell her to take it home, put it on a table, and leave it out overnight so she can check for loose threads. She must fix them Saturday night and bring the cloth back to me Sunday morning."

Lotty was stunned, but she did as she was told. How wonderful it was to have the cloth back in her house for the Sabbath Queen. The following Friday the maid brought Lotty the cloth and gave the same instructions. The arrangement continued for many, many years until the empress died. Lotty wondered if she would ever see her tablecloth again.

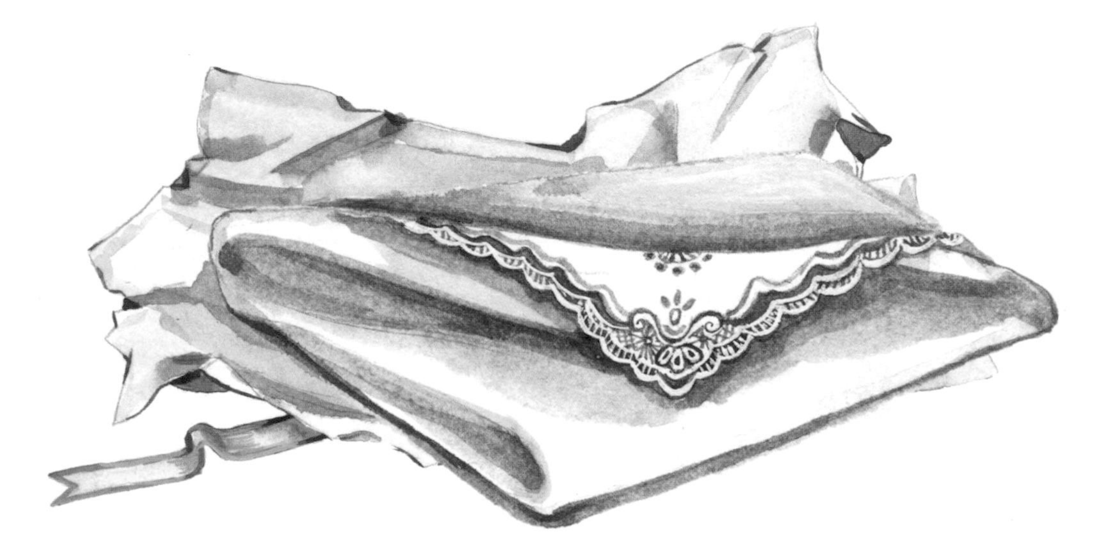

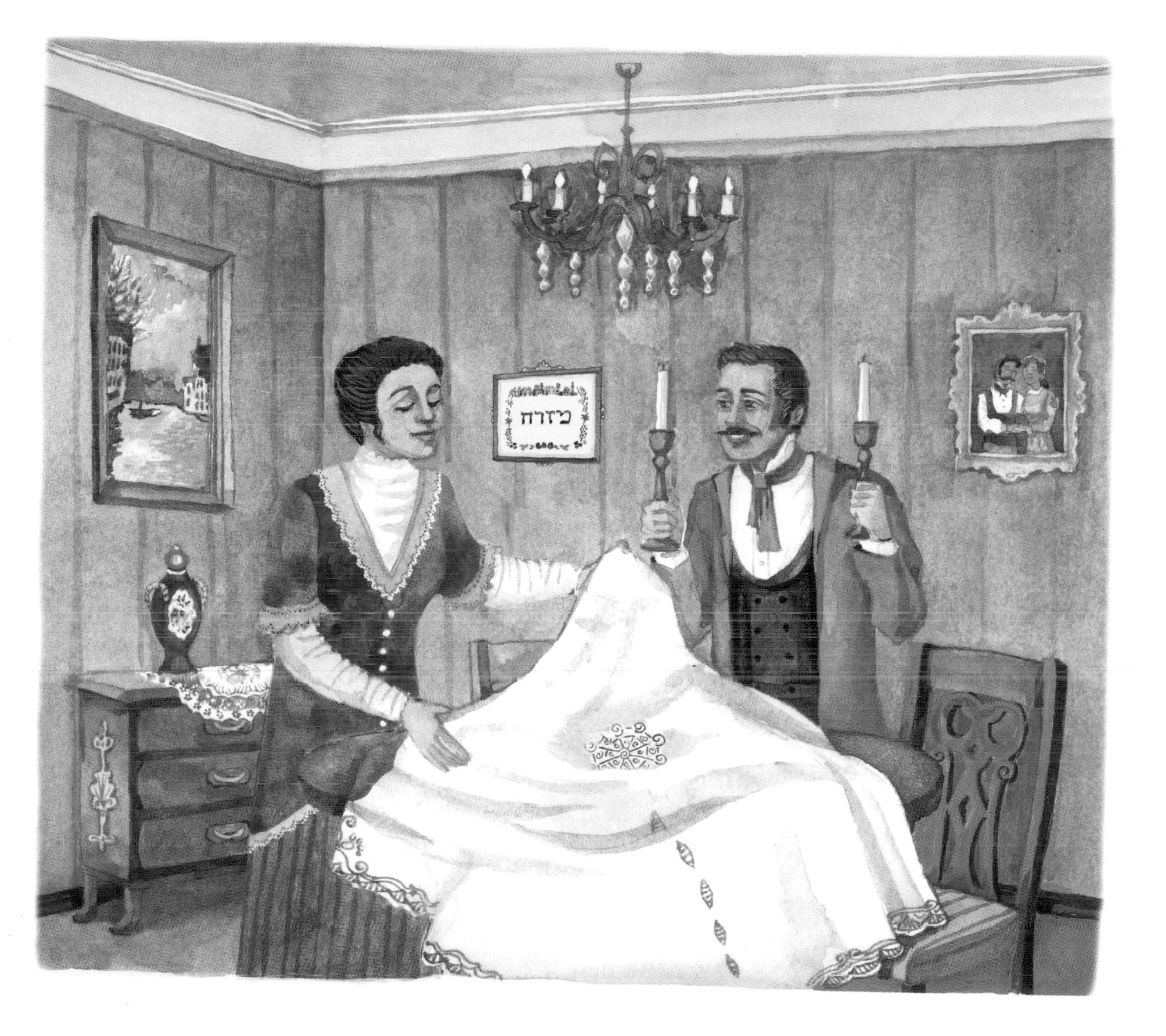
מזרח

A month later a gilded carriage pulled up in front of Lotty's shop. The new empress stepped out. Behind her, a maid carried a large, flat brown box.

"Are you Lotty?" asked the empress, entering the shop.

"I am."

"Then according to my mother's will, this tablecloth is for you." She handed over the box.

Lotty's heart was filled with joy. Carefully fingering the lace, she decided that the tablecloth would stay in her family forever.

Now you know the story of my Great-Great-Great-Grandma Lotty's tablecloth. It has stayed in our family for generations. Grandma says it's time to hand it down. She wants to have the happiness of seeing Mommy use it on Friday nights. Guess what? She also says that someday it will be mine!

This book shows us how the Sabbath – Shabbat – is a day of rest with a unique atmosphere and special items – like the lace tablecloth – dedicated to it. *Is there a family Shabbat heirloom in your house?* A kiddush cup, candlesticks, siddur or a bread plate that has been handed down from one generation to another? Sit down with your mom and dad, or your grandma and grandpa, and write the story of how this heirloom first came into your family. If you have a photo of it, paste it on one of these pages.

ABOUT THE AUTHOR

Tami Lehman-Wilzig is an award-winning children's book author, a cookbook author and one of Israel's leading English language advertising copywriters. Her children's books include *Hlik Lak*, *Tasty Bible Stories* and *Keeping the Promise*, which received a 2005 International Reading Association (IRA) Teachers' Choice Award.

Married to a university professor, and the mother of two grown sons, Tami lives in Petach Tikva, a suburb of Tel Aviv.

ABOUT THE ILLUSTRATOR

Born in Moscow, Ksenia Topaz made aliyah to Israel in 1991. A graduate of Moscow's renowned Strogonoff Academy of Art, Ksenia comes from a family of artists and sculptors. Back in Moscow her home reflected a deep love of children's literature through an extensive collection of illustrated books that enveloped Ksenia in a world of fantasy. Today, Ksenia is a children's book and textbook illustrator who has lent her talents to over 20 books published in Israel. The mother of two daughters, Ksenia lives in Jerusalem.